Crying is Like the Rain

For Orli, my sacred gift. It all began
with you. May the storms of life
deepen your understanding and love of
yourself, widen and open your heart,
and bring you closer to the great
wisdom within. Thank you for sharing
your brilliant light with the world.

— HHF

For my family.
— CK

Crying is Like the Rain

a story of mindfulness and feelings

Heather Hawk Feinberg

Illustrated by
Chamisa Kellogg

TILBURY HOUSE PUBLISHERS, THOMASTON, MAINE

One day I heard
someone special
say, "Feelings are
like the weather.
They come and
they go."

Well, if feelings are like the weather,
then crying is like the rain.

Sometimes people wish the rain wouldn't fall . . .

. . . and sometimes people think crying means something is wrong.

They might say "shhh" or "hush."

Or do something silly to make us laugh.

Sometimes they get worried.

Other times crying hurts their ears or makes them feel scared inside.

But crying is like the rain.

When it's warm outside and the sun is shining softly, the wind is blowing gently, and the clouds are wispy and grand, that's when nature is in balance.

Then there is a shift.

The air becomes too hot or too cold or too dry, and the clouds and the earth send each other messages.

A storm is coming.

Some storms are loud and powerful.
The sky gets dark and rain pours down.

Thunder roars, lightning flashes, and the storm
feels like it will never end, though it always does.

Some storms are small and mild.

The rain may fall even as the sun shines
through the few clouds in the sky.

The rain can be cold and wet and fast,
or sometimes it's light and tickling.

But when it's needed, the rain always comes.

And after the rain pours down, the earth feels fresh and new.

When you are worried or upset, scared or lonely, or something deep within feels off balance, there is a storm building inside you.

The storm may be big or small.

You may feel frustration gathering power like a tornado.

You may feel a red-hot anger growing like the lava in a volcano, ready to explode.

You may feel tidal waves of pressure inside, expanding and pushing out like a hurricane.

You may feel ready to crack wide open like the ground during an earthquake.

You may want to shout like thunder
or lash out like a lightning bolt.

Or you may want to sit still and feel blue,
as if the darkest clouds are hanging over you.

Tears help your mind, your heart, and your body
feel new, clear, and calm after the storm.

We need our tears, just as the earth needs rain.

Feelings aren't meant to be kept inside.

They're meant to be felt, to flow through us like rainwater.

We are not our feelings. Feelings come and go.

Have you ever noticed that after a storm ends,
the earth feels as if it took a big deep breath?

Then we can search for a beautiful rainbow.

It's the same for you and me. Our tears have lessons
to teach us. They connect us to ourselves, deep inside.

We can learn to express and share our
feelings in ways that are safe for everyone.

And then we can look inside for our very own rainbow.

Crying is like the rain.

Crying Really *Is* like the Rain

In my twenty-five years of educating and counseling children, teens, and families, I have seen how powerful the natural world can be for helping us to understand ourselves, our internal lives, and our relationships with one another.

When my own child was a baby and there were oh so many tears, I realized just how uncomfortable we are with crying. I couldn't understand why such a natural and important response to pain, sadness, loss, frustration, sorrow, or anger has the power to disturb us so deeply. Then I discovered the idea that feelings are like the weather, and it changed me. I came to see that tears are teachers, and I was able to put into words what I had always known at some level: Crying is like the rain.

This book is an invitation to look with new eyes at the way we experience feelings—ours and others'—especially the feelings we tend to ignore, hide, or label as wrong or negative. All feelings have a purpose. They guide us toward understanding ourselves and one another. Feelings—big ones, little ones, intense ones—aren't something to fear. Learning how to be with ourselves as we experience feelings—understanding how to weather our inner storms—is an invaluable practice, one we can learn and teach our families. Here are two practices that can help.

Weather Reports: A Mindfulness Game

1. Take a few slow, deep breaths, imagining your breath like a clearing and calming wind.

2. Close your eyes gently and begin to sense what is happening inside you.

3. Notice how you feel. What is your weather? Is it cloudy or rainy? Is the sun shining? Are there big storm clouds? Is it really windy?

4. Notice where the weather is in your body. Is it raining in your heart? Is the sun shining in your belly? The location of our internal weather can help us understand what it has come to teach us and what we need.

5. Now be a weather reporter and share your weather with someone you care about. Sit and be together, tending to whatever the report presents. Remember, we don't need to do anything to change the weather; we can simply welcome it, witness it, and sometimes even ask it questions.

To Go Deeper:

▸ Draw the weather to make it more tangible. Create an outline of a body and hand out crayons or colored pencils so children can illustrate their own inner weather reports.

▸ Explore the concept of inner and outer weather. Children can begin to communicate and sense that the weather inside them can be different from the weather outside—like in their family, with a friend, or at school. This supports healthy emotional boundaries.

▸ Once your family gets comfortable doing weather reports together, use them to connect in the morning before starting the day, in the evening before bed, or in times of transition or challenge. You could simply say, "Would you like to play Weather Reports with me?"

Words Have Power

Being aware of the words we use to communicate with our children during turbulent times is an important part of guiding their development. What we say and how we say it can shape their experience and learning immensely. Share with your children that:

1. All feelings are valid and important. "It's okay to feel _____."

2. They are not alone. You are there to listen, guide them, and keep them safe.
   "I know this is hard. I am here. You are safe."

3. Their feelings will change, just like the weather. "I will be here supporting you as this storm passes through. Let's look for the rainbow together."

It is my hope that this way of being with our feelings will soften us, open us, and allow us to breathe more deeply and feel more fully, knowing that all will pass, and we are safe.

—Heather Hawk Feinberg

Heather Hawk Feinberg (Austin, TX) is a counselor, writer, mother, and the founder of Mindful Kids (www.mindfulkidscommunity.org), a nonprofit organization that creates pioneering resources for social and emotional learning. She works with individuals, families, and organizations across the globe. Heather's calling is guiding children (and the child inside each of us) to discover our voices, access our power, and connect to our knowing. This is her debut book.

Chamisa Kellogg is an illustrator and fine artist who makes art for children's books, editorial publications, and textile design. Chamisa's work seeks to highlight the magic and weirdness of everyday life, drawing inspiration from nature, myths and folklore, and the nebulous line between reality and imagination. Visit her at www.chamisakellogg.com.

Text © 2020 by Heather Hawk Feinberg • Illustrations © 2020 by Chamisa Kellogg • Hardcover ISBN 978-0-88448-723-4 • First hardcover printing April 2020 • Tilbury House Publishers • 12 Starr Street • Thomaston, Maine 04861 • www.tilburyhouse.com • All rights reserved.
No part of this publication may be reproduced or transmitted in any form or by any means, electronic or mechanical, including photocopying, recording, or any information storage or retrieval system, without permission in writing from the publisher. • Library of Congress Control Number: 2020933456 • Designed by Frame25 Productions • Printed in Korea • 15 16 17 18 19 20 XXX 10 9 8 7 6 5 4 3 2 1